This book belongs to:

_____

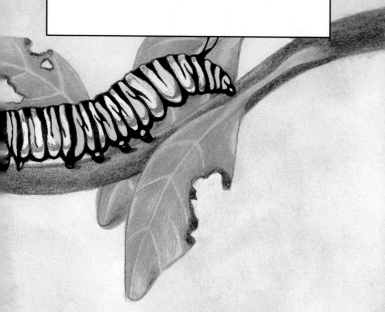

Published by Penguin Books India
11 Community Centre, Panchsheel Park, New Delhi 110017

© PENGUIN BOOKS INDIA 2006

1 3 5 7 9 10 8 6 4 2

Printed at Ajanta Offset & Packagings Ltd, New Delhi

Butterflies

illustrated by Agantuk

Butterflies are colourful flying insects.

These are a few other insects.

7

Butterflies are found all over the world.

9

Butterflies sip nectar from flowers.
They sip the nectar with their long tongue.

tongue

Butterflies have wings that are covered with tiny scales.

scales

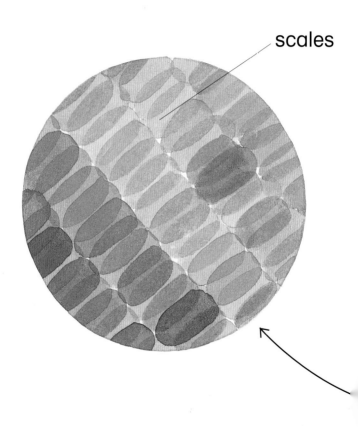

wing

13

Butterflies are brightly
coloured.
Some butterflies have
spots.

15

Butterflies carry pollen from one flower to another. Pollen helps new flowers to grow.

pollen

Butterflies can get hurt
when you catch them.

This butterfly lays her eggs under a leaf.

eggs

A caterpillar comes out of
the egg.

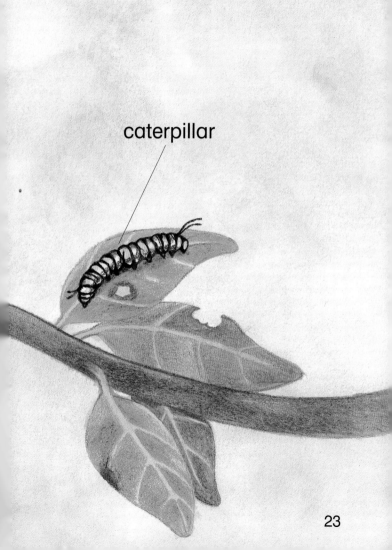

caterpillar

The caterpillar turns into
a pupa.

pupa

A butterfly comes out of the pupa.

27

The butterfly lays eggs
under a leaf.
Do you know what
happens next?

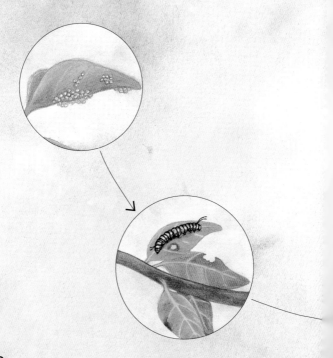

29

Index